GW00858078

This delightful story is about Little Timi the duck exploring the farm and meeting all the farm animals and learning what type of sound they make.

Farm Friends

by Christopher Henderson
Illustrations: by LeRoy Grayson
Published: by Jazzy Kitty Publications

A Fictional Story

FARM FRIENDS

BY CHRISTOPHER HENDERSON

Illustrations by Leroy Grayson

Jazzy Kitty
PUBLICATIONS

This is Timi. Timi is a

Timi's mom told him to go out to play, but not to waddle too far. So Timi waddled away to go and play.

Timi met a black and white

Timi wanted to be friends, so he
asked Who are you?
What sound do you make?

"My name is cow, and I make a
Mooo sound," said the cow.
Timi said, "Nice to meet you!"
as he waddled away to go and play.

Timi then met a brown

Timi wanted to be friends, so he
asked Who are you?
What sound do you make?

"My name is Horse, and I make a
Neigh sound," said the horse.
Timi said, "Nice to meet you!"
as he waddled away to go and play.

Timi then met a white

Timi wanted to be friends, so he
asked Who are you?
What sound do you make?

"My name is Sheep, and I make a
Baa sound," said the sheep.
Timi said, "Nice to meet you!"
as he waddled away to go and play.

Timi then met a pink

Timi wanted to be friends, so he
asked Who are you?
What sound do you make?

"My name is Pig, and I make a
Oink sound," said the pig.
Timi said, "Nice to meet you!"
as he waddled away to go and play.

Timi then met a brown

Timi wanted to be friends, so he
asked Who are you?
What sound do you make?

"My name is Dog, and I make a
Woof sound," said the dog.
Timi said, "Nice to meet you!"
as he waddled away to go and play.

Timi went home and told his mom
about all the farm friends he had

"Mommy, I had so much fun. I
met new friends and I didn't
wander too far."

I met
A cow that goes "moo",
A horse that goes "neigh",
A pig that goes "oink",
A dog that goes "woof",
and a sheep that goes" baa"

Timi's mom was surprised that
Timi had made so many friends.
Timi was tired from all the
waddling.

"Timi, what's wrong?", Asked his mom.
Timi told his mom that he was tired and thirsty, so he decided to get some water by the lake. While going to the lake, Timi stumbled upon the farm animals Timi said "Hi" and so did his friends.

They asked him, Hello friend,
What is your name, and what
sound do you make?
I'm Timi, and I go
Quack!
Quack!
Quack!
He then waddled away to the
lake.

The End

This book is dedicated to God, my family, and friends.

I want to say thank you to my grandfather Lero Grayson for his ability to illustrate my vision.

My mother for her inspiration in helping me t complete this book.

Also, my publisher Anelda Attaway.

18

rm Friends

y Christopher Henderson

ustrations by Leroy Grayson

ublished by Jazzy Kitty Publications

ew Castle, DE 19720

7.782.5550 - http://www.jazzykittypublications.com

elda@jazzykittypublications.com

BN 978-1-954425-31-6

brary of Congress Control Number: 2021910976

edits: Cover image and illustrations by Leroy Grayson of Quality Pictures qualitypictures2@aol.com; Book ver created and Editing by Anelda Attaway Co-editor Leroy Grayson; Logo Designs by Andre M. Saunders d Jess Zimmerman.

CPSIA information can be obtained
at www.ICGtesting.com
Printed in the USA
BVHW011036160621
609723BV00018B/364